For Charlotte, with all
my love xx - T.C.

For Matt, Lou and Marcie - J.C.

tiger tales
5 River Road, Suite 128, Wilton, CT 06897
Published in the United States 2014
Originally published in Great Britain 2014
by Little Tiger Press
Text copyright © 2014 Tracey Corderoy
Illustrations copyright © 2014 Jane Chapman
Visit Jane Chapman at www.ChapmanandWarnes.com
ISBN-13: 978-1-58925-162-5
ISBN-10: 1-58925-162-8
Printed in China
LTP/1400/0893/0314
10 9 8 7 6 5 4 3 2 1

For more insights and activities, visit us at www.tigertalesbooks.com

THE MAGICAL
SNOW GARDEN

by Tracey Corderoy

Illustrated by Jane Chapman

tiger tales

Far away, where
snowflakes twinkled, lived
a little penguin named Wellington.
Wellington loved his snowy world—
sliding down hills, digging for treasure, and
sharing books with his very best friend.
"Rosemary, look at this **garden**," he cried.
"It's amazing! Let's grow one just like it!"

"PERCY!" called Wellington. "I'm going to grow a garden!"

"Oh, Wellington," chuckled Percy, "that's impossible!"

"We don't grow things! We fish," Mabel smiled.

"I wanted to fly once," Ivan explained. "But penguins **can't** fly. And flowers **can't** grow in the snow—it's just **too** cold!"

"But **Ivan**," said Wellington, "how will we know unless we **try**?"

Wellington's books all said the same
thing: To grow flowers, he needed seeds.
But there weren't any seeds in their
snowy, white world. Not one.
"There MUST be a way," Rosemary
chirped as they shared a cookie.

Wellington looked at the shiny, blue wrapper.

With a fold here and there, it was just like . . .

"A tulip!" cried Wellington. "I can **make** a garden instead!"

So Wellington filled his biggest
net with things to make his
garden: wrappers, buttons, pieces
of Ivan's old clocks, and pearly-
white seashells that Rosemary
had given him.

For **days**, Wellington raced around—folding and twirling . . .

glittering and gluing . . .

digging and planting, **until** . . .

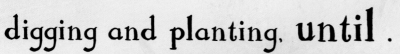

"Ta daaa!"

Now all of the wrappers
were beautiful flowers, and the
buttons were bright bumblebees.
Clockwork trees dotted the hills,
sprinkled with soft white snow.

"Look!" Percy pointed.
"Wow!" Mabel gasped.
"HE'S DONE IT!"
Ivan smiled.

"Wellington's made a **magical snow** garden!" they cried.

But the garden had no wall
to keep out the wind. And that
very night a storm blew in.
It whipped and whirled and
roared. WHOOSH!

And Wellington's garden was blown away . . .

. . . every last petal.

"It's okay." said Mabel. "You tried your best."

They brought him warm milk and cookies. But Wellington shook his head. "No thanks," he sighed.

Just then, he heard a flutter of wings, and Rosemary dropped something in his lap.

Slowly, Wellington smoothed out the shiny blue wrapper. Then he folded it, just so.

"The first tulip for my **next** garden!" Wellington decided.

This time, Wellington's friends helped to make his wonderful new garden.

Percy built a wall to keep out the wind, Mabel made a beautiful fountain, and Ivan's trees had clockwork birds that sang!

Then Rosemary flew off to tell the world about her friend's **amazing garden . . .**

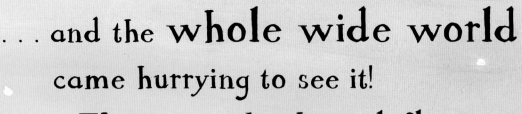

. . . and the **whole wide world**
came hurrying to see it!
There were bright pink flamingos,
koalas, and camels, and elephants with
trumpeting trunks.
There were zebras, giraffes, and
bouncing kangaroos!
"**Wow!**" Wellington gasped.

"Wellington!" called Ivan. "You were right! You never know **what** you can do until you **try!**"

"**Hooray** for Wellington," everyone cheered, "and his **magical garden** in the **snow!**"